Enid Blyton

A WISHING-CHAIR ADVENTURE

A SUMMERTIME MYSTER

D0263442

For Lauren and Neve
A. P.

HODDER CHILDREN'S BOOKS
Text first published in Great Britain as chapters 10, 16 and 17 of
The Adventures of the Wishing-Chair in 1937
First published as *A Summertime Mystery: A Wishing-Chair Adventure* in 2019
by Egmont UK Limited
This edition published in 2021 by Hodder & Stoughton Limited

1 3 5 7 9 10 8 6 4 2

Enid Blyton ® and Enid Blyton's signature are registered trade marks of Hodder & Stoughton Limited
Text © 2021 Hodder & Stoughton Limited
Cover and interior illustrations by Alex Paterson. Illustrations © 2021 Hodder & Stoughton Limited

No trade mark or copyrighted material may be reproduced without the express written permission
of the trade mark and copyright owner.
The moral right of the author has been asserted.

All characters and events in this publication, other than those clearly
in the public domain, are fictitious and any resemblance to
real persons, living or dead, is purely coincidental.

All rights reserved.
No part of this publication may be reproduced, stored in
a retrieval system, or transmitted, in any form or by any means, without
the prior permission in writing of the publisher, nor be otherwise circulated
in any form of binding or cover other than that in which it is published
and without a similar condition including this condition being
imposed on the subsequent purchaser.

A CIP catalogue record for this book is available from the British Library.

ISBN 978 1 444 96238 3

Printed and bound in China

The paper and board used in this book are made from wood from responsible sources.

Hodder Children's Books
An imprint of
Hachette Children's Group
Part of Hodder & Stoughton
Carmelite House
50 Victoria Embankment
London EC4Y 0DZ

An Hachette UK Company
www.hachette.co.uk
www.hachettechildrens.co.uk

Enid Blyton

A WISHING-CHAIR ADVENTURE

A SUMMERTIME MYSTERY

HODDER

THE WISHING-CHAIR – what magical adventure will it take the children on next?

The playroom at the bottom of the garden is where nearly all the wishing-chair's adventures begin . . .

PETER

MOLLIE

BINKY is the most helpful pixie you ever did meet

CHAPTER ONE
THE DISAPPEARING ISLAND

It happened once that the children and Binky had a most unpleasant adventure, and it was all Mollie's fault.

The wishing-chair grew its wings one bright sunny morning just as the three of them were planning a game of pirates. Mollie saw the red wings **growing** from the legs of the chair and cried out in delight.

'Look! The chair's off again! Let's get in and have an **adventure**!'

They all crowded into it, and in a trice the chair was off through the door and into the air. It was such fun, for the day was clear and sunny, and the children could see for miles.

The chair flew on and on, and came to the towers and spires of **Fairyland**. They glittered in the sun and Peter wanted to go down and visit the Prince and Princess they had once rescued. But the chair still flew on. It flew over the **Land of Gnomes**, and over the Land of Toadstools, and at last came to a bright blue sea.

'Hallo, hallo!' said Binky, peering over the edge of the chair. 'I've never been as far as this before. I don't know if we ought to fly over the sea. The chair might get **tired** – and then what would happen to us if we all came down in the sea!'

'We shan't do that!' said Mollie, pointing to a blue island far away on the horizon. 'I think the chair is making for that land over there.'

The chair flew steadily towards it, and the children saw that the land they had seen in the distance was a small and **beautiful** island. It was packed with flowers, and the sound of bells came faintly up from the fields and hills.

'We mustn't go there,' said Binky suddenly.

'That's **Disappearing Island**!'

'Well, why shouldn't we go there?' said Mollie.

'Because it suddenly disappears,' said Binky. 'I've heard of it before. It's a horrid place. You get there and think it's all as beautiful as can be – and then it suddenly disappears and takes you with it.'

'It can't be horrid,' said Mollie longingly, looking down at the sunny, flower-spread island. 'Oh, Binky, you must be mistaken. It's the **most** beautiful island I ever saw! I do want to go. There are some lovely birds there too. I can hear them singing.'

'I tell you, Mollie, it's dangerous to go to Disappearing Island,' said Binky crossly. 'You might believe me.'

'You're not always right!' said Mollie

obstinately. 'I *want* to go there! Wishing-chair, fly down to that lovely island.'

At once the chair began to fly **downwards**. Binky glared at Mollie, but the words were said. He couldn't unsay them. Down they flew and down and down!

The **brilliant** island came nearer and nearer. Mollie shouted in delight to see such glorious

bright flowers, such shiny-winged birds, such plump, soft rabbits. The chair flew **swiftly** towards them.

And then, just as they were about to land in a field spread with buttercups as large as poppies, among soft-eyed **bunnies** and singing birds, a most strange and peculiar thing happened.

The island disappeared! One moment it was there, and the sun was shining on its fields – and the next moment there was only a faint blue mist! The chair flew through the mist – and then *splash*! They were all in the sea!

CHAPTER TWO
A WATERY SURPRISE

Mollie and Peter were flung off the chair into the water. Binky grabbed the back of the chair, and reached his hand out to the children. They clambered back on to the chair, which was **bobbing** about on the waves, soaking wet.

Binky turned to Mollie. 'What did I tell you?' he said angrily. 'Didn't I say it was Disappearing Island? Now see what's happened! It's gone and disappeared, and we've fallen into the sea! A nice pickle we are in – all wet and **shivery**!'

Mollie went red. How she wished she hadn't wanted to go to Disappearing Island!

'Well, I didn't know it was going to disappear so suddenly,' she said. 'I'm very sorry.'

'Not much good being sorry,' said Peter gloomily, **squeezing** the water out of his clothes. 'How are we going to get to land? As far as I can see there is water all round us for miles! The chair's wings are wet, and it can't fly.'

The three of them were indeed in a **dreadful** fix! It was fortunate for them that the chair was made of wood, or they would not have had anything to cling to!

They bobbed **up** and **down** for some time, wondering what to do. Suddenly, to their great surprise, a little head popped out of the sea.

'Hallo!' it said. 'Are you wanting help?'

'Yes,' said Binky. 'Are you a merman?'

'I am!' said the little fellow. The children looked down at him, and through the water they could see his fish-like body covered with **scales** from the waist downwards and ending in a silvery tail. 'Do you want to be towed to land?'

'Yes, please,' said Binky joyfully.

'That will cost you a **piece of gold**,' said the merman.

'I haven't any with me, but we will send it to you as soon as we get home,' promised Binky.

The merman swam off and came back riding on a **big** fish. He threw a rope of seaweed around the back of the chair and **shouted** to Binky to hold on to it.

Then the fish set off at a great speed, towing the chair behind it with Binky and the children safely on it! The merman rode on the fish all the way, singing a **funny** little watery song. It was a strange ride!

Soon they came to land, and the children
dragged the chair out of the water on to the
sunbaked sand.

'Thank you,' they said to the merman. 'We
will send you the money as soon as we can.'

The merman **jumped** on the fish again,
waved his wet hand, and dived into the waves
with a splash.

'We'll wait till the sun has dried the chair's wings, and we'll dry our own clothes,' said Binky. 'Then we'll go home. I think that was a most unpleasant **adventure**. We might have been bobbing about for days on the sea!'

Mollie didn't say anything. She knew it was all her fault.

They dried their clothes, and as soon as the wings of the chair were quite dry too, they sat in it, and Binky cried, 'Home, **wishing-chair**, home!'

They flew home.

Mollie **jumped** off the chair as soon as it arrived in the playroom and ran to her money-box. She tipped out all her money.

'Here you are, Binky,' she said. 'I'm going to pay for that fish-ride myself. It was all my fault. I'm very **sorry**, and I won't be so silly again. Do forgive me!'

'Oh! That's very nice of you, Mollie!' said Binky, and he gave her a hug. 'Of course we

forgive you! All's well that ends well! We're
home again **safe** and sound!'

He changed Mollie's money into a big
gold piece and gave it to the blackbird in the
garden, asking him to take it to the merman.

'That's the end of *that* adventure!' said Binky.
'Well, let's hope our next one will be much,
much nicer!'

CHAPTER THREE
THE SILLY BOY

The children were cross because Mother had said that the painters were to paint the walls of the **playroom** and mend a window – and this meant that they couldn't play there for some time.

Their playroom was built right at the bottom of the garden, and it was quite safe for their friend, Binky the **pixie**, to live there, for no one ever went to the garden playroom except themselves. But now the painters would be there for a week. How tiresome!

'It's a good thing it's **summertime**, Binky, so that you can live in the garden for a bit,' said Mollie.

'Oh, don't worry about *me*,' said Binky. 'I've a nice **cosy** place in the hollow of an oak tree. It's the chair I'm thinking about. Where shall we keep that? We can't have it flying about whilst the painters are there.'

'We'd better put it in the boxroom, indoors,' said Peter. 'That room's just been repainted so I don't expect Mother or anyone will think it must be turned out just yet. It will be safe there.'

So, when no one was **looking**, Peter and Mollie carried the wishing-chair up to the boxroom and stood it safely in a corner. They shut the window up tightly, so that it couldn't fly out if its wings **grew** suddenly.

They couldn't have Binky to play with them in the house, because he didn't want anyone to know about him. So they asked Thomas,

the little boy over the road, to come and play
soldiers, on a **rainy** afternoon. They didn't like
him very much, but he was better than nobody.

Thomas came. He soon got tired of playing
soldiers. He began turning **head-over-heels**
down the nursery floor.
He could do it
very well.

'I can make **awful** faces, too,' he said to Mollie and Peter – and he began to pull such dreadful faces that the two children gazed at him in **surprise** and horror.

'Our mother says that if you pull faces and the wind happens to change you may get stuck like that,' said Mollie. 'Do stop it, Thomas.'

But Thomas wouldn't. He wrinkled up his nose and his forehead and blew out his cheeks

– and do you know, the wind **changed** that very minute! And poor Thomas couldn't get his face right again! He tried and he tried, but he couldn't. It was dreadful! Whatever was he to do?

'Oh, Thomas, the **wind** changed – I saw the weather-cock swing round that very moment!' cried Mollie. 'I did warn you! I do think you're silly.'

'He can't go home like that,' said Peter. 'Let's wash his face in hot water – then perhaps it will go right again.'

So they washed Thomas's face well – but it was as bad as ever when they had finished! Screwed-up nose and forehead and blown-out cheeks . . . oh dear!

CHAPTER FOUR
WHATEVER NEXT?

'Do you suppose Binky would know what to do?' said Peter at last.

'Who's Binky?' asked Thomas.

'Never you mind,' said Mollie. 'Peter, go and find Binky and see what he says. I'll stay here with Thomas. He mustn't go out of the nursery, because if he meets Mother or Jane, they will think he's making faces at them and will be ever so cross.'

Peter ran downstairs. He went into the garden and whistled a little tune that Binky had

taught him. He had to whistle this whenever
he wanted the pixie.

Binky whistled back. Peter saw him under a
big hawthorn bush, mending a hole in his coat.

'What's up?' asked Binky, sewing away.

'We've got a boy in our nursery who's been making **dreadful** faces,' explained Peter. 'And the wind changed just as he was making a specially horrible one – and now he can't get his face right again. So Mollie sent me to ask you if you could do anything to help.'

'A boy as **silly** as that doesn't deserve help,' said Binky, breaking off his cotton and threading his needle again. 'You go and tell him so.'

'Oh no, Binky, we really must help him,' said Peter. 'His mother may think we made his face like that, and we'll get into **trouble**. You don't want us to be sent to bed for a week, do you?'

'No, I don't,' said Binky, putting on his coat. 'I'll help you because you're my friends. There's only one thing to be done for a person who's been making faces when the wind changed.'

'What's that?' asked Peter.

'You've got to get a bit of the wind that **blew** just then, and puff it into his face,' said Binky. 'Then he'll be all right – but it's dreadfully difficult to get a bit of the same wind.'

'How can we?' asked Peter, in dismay.

'We'd better go in the **wishing-chair** to the **Windy Wizard**,' said Binky. 'He knows all the ins and outs of every wind that blows. I've seen the old wishing-chair looking out of the window this afternoon, trying to get out, so I'm sure it's grown its wings again. Go and see, and if it has, tell Mollie, and we'll go and get help from the old **wizard**.'

'Oh, thank you, Binky,' said Peter, and he ran indoors.

He **whispered** to Mollie all that Binky had said.

'I think the chair must have **grown** its wings,' Mollie said, 'because there have been such strange sounds going on in the boxroom this afternoon – you know, **knockings** and **bumping**. I expect it's the chair trying to get out.'

'I'll go and see,' said Peter.

He ran up the top-most flight of stairs and opened the boxroom door. The wishing-chair was standing by it, ready to fly out — but Peter caught hold of it just as it was slipping out of the door.

'Now just **wait** a minute,' he said.

But the chair wouldn't! It forced its way past Peter and the little boy jumped into it.

'**Go to Binky!**' he called, hoping that the chair wouldn't meet any one on the way.

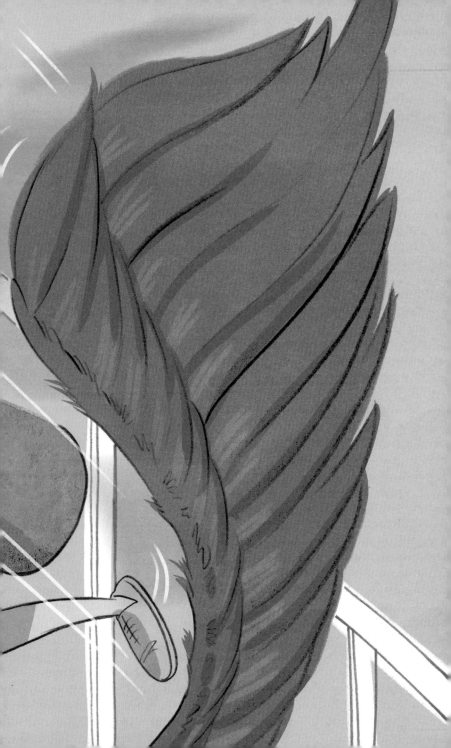

The chair flew **down** the stairs and out into the garden. It went to where Binky was standing by the hawthorn bush. It was **flapping** its red wings madly and Binky jumped into it at once.

'To the **Windy Wizard's**!' he shouted. 'I say, Peter, isn't it in a hurry! It must have got tired of being shut up in the boxroom!'

Mollie was **looking** out of the window. She had heard the chair flying downstairs. She saw it up in the air, carrying Peter and Binky, and she wished she were in it too!

'Someone's got to stay with Thomas, though,' she thought to herself. 'He'd only run home or go and find our mother or something, if we left him quite alone. What an ugly face he has now! I do hope Peter and Binky find something to put it right!'

CHAPTER FIVE
THE WINDY WIZARD

The wishing-chair rose **high** into the air, carrying Peter and Binky. It was a **hot** sunny day and the wind the chair made rushing through the air was very pleasant. Peter wished Mollie was with them. It was much more fun to go on adventures all together.

Presently the chair came into a very **windy** sky. Goodness, how the wind blew! It blew the white clouds to rags. It blew Peter's hair nearly off his head! It **blew** the chair's wings so that it could hardly flap them.

'The **Windy Wizard** lives somewhere about here,' said Binky, looking down. '**Look!** Do you see that hill over there, golden with buttercups? There's a house there. It's the Windy Wizard's, I'm sure, because it's **rocking** about in all directions as if the wind lived inside it!'

Down flew the wishing-chair. It came to rest outside the cottage, which was certainly **rocking** about in a most alarming manner. Peter and Binky jumped off and ran to the cottage door. They knocked.

'**Come in!**' cried a voice.

They opened the door and went in. Oooh! The wind rushed out at them and nearly blew them off their feet!

'Good-day!' said the Windy Wizard. He was a most **peculiar-looking** person, for he had long hair and a very long beard and a cloak that swept to the ground, but, as the wind blew his hair and beard and cloak up and down and round and about all the time, it was very difficult to see what he was really like!

'Good-day,' said Peter and Binky, staring
at the wizard. He hadn't a very comfortable
house to live in, Peter thought, because there
were draughts everywhere, round his legs,
down his neck, behind his knees! And all the
cottage was full of a whispering, sighing sound
as if a wind was talking to itself all the time.

'Have you come to buy a little wind?'

asked the wizard.

'No,' said Binky. 'I've come about a boy who made faces when the wind changed – and he can't get right again. So we thought perhaps you could help us. I know that if we could get a little of the wind that blew at that time, and puff it into his face, he'll be all right – but how can we get the wind?'

'What a foolish boy!' said the Windy Wizard, his cloak blowing out and **hiding** him completely. 'What time did this happen?'

'At half-past three this afternoon,' said Peter. 'I heard the nursery clock strike.'

'It's difficult, very difficult,' said the wizard, smoothing down his cloak. 'You see, the wind **blows** and is gone in a trice! Now let me think for a moment – who is likely to have kept a little of that wind?'

'What about the birds that were flying in the air at that moment?' asked Binky. 'They may have some in their feathers, you know.'

'Yes, so they may,' said the wizard. He took a feather from a jar that was full of them, and flung it out of the door.

'Come, birds, and bring
The breeze from your wing!'

he chanted.

Peter and Binky
looked out of the
door, hoping that
dozens of birds would
come – but only one
appeared, and that
was a blackbird.

CHAPTER SIX
CATCHING THE BREEZE

'Only one bird was flying in the air with the wind at that moment,' said the wizard. 'Come, blackbird, shake your feathers. I want the wind from them!'

The blackbird shook his glossy feathers out

and the wizard held a green paper bag under them to catch the wind in them. The bag blew up a little, like a balloon.

'Not enough wind here to change your friend's face back again!' said the wizard, looking at it. 'I wonder if there were any kites using the wind at that moment!'

He went to a cupboard and took the tail of a kite out of it. He threw it up into the air just outside the door.

'Come, kites, and bring
The breeze from your wing!'

he called.

Peter and Binky watched eagerly – and to their delight saw two kites sailing down from the sky. One was a green one and one was a red. They fell at the wizard's feet.

He shook each one to get the wind into his green bag.

It blew up just a little more.

'Still not enough,' said the wizard. 'I'll get the little ships along. There will surely be enough then!'

He ran to the mantelpiece and took a tiny sailor doll from it. He threw it up into the air and it disappeared.

'*Come, ships, and bring*
The breeze from your wing!'

sang the old wizard, his hair and beard streaming out like smoke.

Then, sailing up a tinkling stream that ran

down the hillside came six little toy **sailing ships**, their sails full of the wind. They sailed right up to the wizard's front door, for the stream suddenly seemed to run there – and quickly and neatly the old wizard seized each ship, shook its sails into the green paper bag, and then popped it back on the stream. Away sailed the ships again and Peter and Binky saw them no more.

The paper bag was quite fat and **full** now.

'That's about enough, I think,' said the wizard. 'Now I'll put the wind into a pair of bellows for you!'

He took a small pair of bellows from his fire-side and put the tip of them into the green paper bag. He opened the bellows and they sucked in all the air from the bag. The wizard handed them to Peter and Binky.

'Now don't puff with these **bellows** until you reach your friend,' he said. 'Then use them hard and puff all the air into his face! It will come right again in a twink!'

'Thank you so much for your help,' said Binky gratefully.

He and Peter ran to the **wishing-chair** again and climbed into it, holding the bellows carefully. The chair rose up into the air as Binky cried, **'Home, chair, home!'**

In a few minutes it was flying in at the
boxroom window, for Mollie had run up and
opened it, ready for the chair when it came
back again. Peter and Binky shut the window
after them, ran down to the nursery and **burst**
in at the door.

Thomas was still there, his face **screwed up** and his cheeks blown out!

'I'm so glad you're back!' said Mollie. 'It's horrid being here with Thomas. His face is so nasty to look at, it makes me feel I'm in a dream! Have you got something to make it right?'

'Yes,' said Binky, showing her the bellows. 'The Windy Wizard has filled these bellows full of the wind that blew when Thomas made that face. If we puff it at him, his face will be all right again!'

'Go on then, puff!' said Mollie.

So Binky lifted up the bellows and puffed them right into Thomas's face – phooooof! Thomas gasped and spluttered. He shut his eyes and coughed – and when he opened them, his face had gone right again! His nose and

forehead were no longer screwed up, and his cheeks were quite **flat**, not a bit blown up!

'You're right again now, Thomas,' said Binky. 'But let it be a **lesson** to you not to be silly any more.'

'I'll never pull faces again,' said Thomas, who had really had a dreadful fright. 'But who are you? Are you a **fairy**?'

'Never mind who I am, and don't say a word about me or what has happened this afternoon!' said Binky, and Thomas promised. He **ran** home feeling puzzled, but very happy to think that he had got his face its **right** shape again.

'Well, that was an **exciting** sort of adventure, Mollie!' said Peter, and he told her all about it. 'The **Windy Wizard** was so nice. I say – what about giving him back his bellows?'

'I'll manage that,' said Binky, taking them. 'I must go now or someone will come into the nursery and see me! Good-bye till next time!'

THE MAGIC FARAWAY TREE

Enid Blyton
A FARAWAY TREE ADVENTURE
A colour short story

The Land of
BIRTHDAYS

Enid Blyton
A FARAWAY TREE ADVENTURE
A colour short story
Illustrated by Alex Paterson

The Land of MAGIC
MEDICINES

Enid Blyton
A FARAWAY TREE ADVENTURE
A colour short story
Illustrated by Alex Paterson

The Land of
DO-AS-YOU-PLEASE

Enid Blyton
A FARAWAY TREE ADVENTURE
A colour short story
Illustrated by Alex Paterson

The Land of
TOYS

Enid Blyton
A FARAWAY TREE ADVENTURE
A colour short story
Illustrated by Alex Paterson

The Land of
ENCHANTMENTS

Collect all the magical
Faraway Tree Adventures – packed full
of exciting new colour illustrations!

THE WISHING-CHAIR ADVENTURES

Get whisked away on a magical adventure by one of the world's best-loved storytellers

Enid Blyton
A WISHING-CHAIR ADVENTURE
THE ROYAL BIRTHDAY

Enid Blyton
A WISHING-CHAIR ADVENTURE
OFF ON A HOLIDAY ADVENTURE

Enid Blyton
A WISHING-CHAIR ADVENTURE
A DARING SCHOOL RESCUE

Enid Blyton
A WISHING-CHAIR ADVENTURE
THE WITCH'S LOST CAT

Enid Blyton
A WISHING-CHAIR ADVENTURE
HOME FOR HALF-TERM

hodder HODDER